LAVENDER

AMONG THE DAFFODILS

Kim Saynor-Lomas

DEDICATED TO THE MEMORY OF BONNIE.

In remembrance of all the dogs who have died on evil puppy farms

And with compassion for those

Who are still suffering now...

Needing to be rescued by those who dedicate their lives to ending puppy farming, and the rescuers; and to the fosterers who care for those rescued until forever loving homes are found for them...

May they see the sea, walk on grass and know love for the first time in their lives once they are physically healed... The mental scars remain with them for the rest of their lives, but we must never give up hope that they will learn to trust, decent human beings...

COME SIT ON MY RAINBOW WHERE GOLD-DUST APPEARS

YOUR PROBLEM BE DEALT WITH – 'TWILL ALL BECOME CLEAR

TUDOR CHOPS

Tudor Chops was sulking. Mr. Chops, the Elf who owned the butchers shop in Withernsea had told him it was time he didn't eat so much, because he was putting on weight!

Tudor saw himself as a fine St. Bernard dog. He was a good guard dog as well at night for the butcher's shop, where he lived with his adopters, Kate and Sidney Chops.

Secretly, Tudor had been creeping into the back of the shop where all the fresh meat was delivered and prepared for selling by Mr. Chops!

If Mr. Chops happened to drop one of his home made beef and

tomato sausages, Tudor would sneak under the butchers block and 'retrieve' the said sausage; telling himself he was merely trying to help Mr. Chops clean up the floor!

Tudor's favourites were the ones containing tomato flavouring mixed with the minced beef. After retrieving the dropped sausages, Tudor would go and hide whilst he ate them; drooling the whole time as he chomped!

Mr. Chops believed this was the reason Tudor was gaining weight too much and too quickly. Tudor was getting rounder by the day in his tummy. Mr. Chops as much as he tried, could never catch Tudor in the act, to tell him that it was bad for him.

One evening, Kate and Sidney Chops were sat by the log fire after their evening meal. They did not realize that Tudor was hiding behind the curtains, and he was listening to their conversation. Tudor often hid there; he said to himself that it was the only way he could find out things!

"That dog will eat us out of house and home; it's about time we took stock and did something about it!" said Mr. Chops.

Mrs. Chops looked at Mr. Chops...

"We could always 'send him to Coventry'!" said Mrs. Chops; with a smile on her face that Tudor could not see as she had her back to him.

Mr. Chops thought for a while...

"Yes you're right Kate!" said Mr. Chops "we will deal with him first thing in the morning; I believe he is downstairs now guarding the shop!"

Mrs. Chops chuckled "more likely he is fast asleep down there Sidney!

Tudor began to worry, and his mind was racing in turmoil. He did not want to be sent to Coventry; in fact he had no idea where Coventry was, and nor had he ever heard of the place!

Tudor Chops spent most of that night thinking hard, whilst he was guarding the butcher's shop downstairs.

Tudor was talking to himself under his breath...

"They're not sending me to NO Coventry; I know where I am not wanted anymore!"

Tudor decided to pack his rucksack full of the freshly delivered meat that had been delivered early the day before. He gathered plenty of complete dog mixture as he possibly could fit in the rucksack. It was fit to bursting when Tudor managed to fasten it, by pulling on the cords. He then sneaked to the shelf, knocked the bottle of medicinal brandy off the shelf, pulled out its cork with his teeth and filled his keg barrel which was around his neck on his collar. Tudor sneaked out into the moonlight, without making a sound...

Tudor Chops found himself walking in very heavy early spring rain. He was thinking to himself wondering if his family would even notice he had gone...

It seemed a very long time had passed since he left his warm and safe home in

Withernsea...

The sun had risen, and all the puddles had lovely bright colours in them. Tudor remembered back to when he was a puppy; running and splashing in them, after Kate and Sidney Chops had adopted him from the shelter, and took him home. Tudor could not believe he was going to live with someone who made sausages.
 He missed his own Mummy at first, but at least she had been found

a lovely home with some kind people in Hornsea, who didn't want a puppy. They had wanted to re home an older dog. They had waited patiently for someone to adopt Tudor, before they took his Mummy away from him.

Tudor stopped for a while and stared at the pretty patterns which were forming in the water filled holes. He was soaked through to the skin, and he shook himself as a man with a pink poodle passed by him...

"Get away you big flea ridden mongrel!" said the man to Tudor. "There there Fifi, the nasty dog has dirtied all your lovely pink fur!"

The man stamped his foot at Tudor and Tudor thought it was best to run as fast as he could. The weight of his rucksack was making his back very sore indeed!

Over the following week, Tudor would get on buses by pretending he was with human's or Elves, who were getting on at the same time as he was; each journey would always end the same, with him being thrown off the buses because he was found out and had no money to pay his fare.

Tudor walked for many a mile; he had no clue where he now was...

A strange sound was beginning to come through to his big floppy ears...

Tudor Chops realized it was some sort of ferry port. He had seen boats before on the sea at Withernsea, on outings with Mr. Chops. Mrs. Chops would often meet them at the lighthouse after she had done her shopping.

Tudor got some meat from his rucksack and had what he considered to be an 'elegant sufficiency'!

A voice called out in distress:

"Help please somebody help me!"

Tudor looked round to see an Elf laid on the floor. The Elf appeared to be dazed and was cut and bruised!

Tudor ran over to the Elf; knowing the Elf would be able to understand dog talk.

Tudor asked the Elf what had happened. The Elf could hardly speak!

"I think you're in shock Mr. Elf!" said Tudor Chops.

Tudor shook his head until his medicinal brandy keg freed itself from around his neck. The Elf was so grateful; and as he took a few sips he began to stop trembling and bring himself round to make himself coherent...

"I was just deciding whether to get two tickets for the boat over to Ireland, for me and my little dog Poppy to make a fresh start in our lives, after my wife passed away a few weeks ago; when I was wrestled to the ground all of a sudden without warning from behind. I thought he wanted my money, but I still have it!" said the Elf.

"What dog Mr. Elf?" asked Tudor.

The Elf looked about him... "Oh no, my faithful companion has been stolen!" said the Elf.

Tudor Chops went for a good look around. He went in search in all the nearby bushes in case Poppy was in hiding frightened; but no dog was in the surrounding area. He went back to the Elf with the bad news...

"It looks like your dog may have left on the last ferry Mr. Elf. I have sniffed your coat and followed the trail as far as the platform to the ferry dock area!" said Tudor.

The Elf had by now much recovered and was behaving very sensibly again after

his ordeal...

"What's your name my kind dog?" asked the Elf.

"Tudor Chops Mr. Elf!" answered Tudor.
"Oh, you can call me Uncle Pogle Tudor!" said the Elf "everybody else does who knows me!"

"I'm very pleased to meet you Uncle Pogle!" said Tudor.
"Have you no home Tudor?" asked Uncle Pogle.

"I did Uncle Pogle yes, but they didn't want me and I don't want to talk about it anymore, if that is alright with you!" said Tudor.

"That is fine by me Tudor. Would you like to go on the ferry with me over to Ireland? I have no choice now other than to go and try to find my little dog Poppy!" said Uncle Pogle.

"I would like that very much Uncle Pogle!" said Tudor. They boarded the ferry to Dublin, after getting two tickets with no return...

O'SEANESSY

Uncle Pogle and Tudor, got off the ferry wondering wherever to begin searching for Poppy.

An old Elf was sat at a table at the Shamrock Inn. He watched them intently while he was drinking his tankard of O'Guinessy, and eating his ploughman's lunch. He spoke with a very broad Irish accent...

"Can I be helping you me fellow?" asked the Elf. "Me name is O'Seanessy, to be sure it is!"

Uncle Pogle walked over to the old Elf and Tudor Chops followed him. After proper introductions they told O'Seanessy all about what had happened when Poppy had been stolen.

"Well Pogle, can I be calling you Pogle me fellow? You're not old enough to be me Uncle; to be sure you are not. I think I may be of some help there to be sure I do!" said O'Seanessy. "I do be sitting here most days a minding me own business, and today I watched some very strange goings on, so I did, aye so I did!"

Old O'Seanessy went on to tell Uncle Pogle how he had watched a fine and dandy looking Elf get out of a big white van with a beautiful Lhasa apso girl dog, who had looked so afraid of him, and how they had boarded the ferry and left the van in the lay by...

"She was a little beauty!" said O'Seanessy "and by the looks of her she had not long had her puppies!"

"Why do you think that was strange O'Seanessy?" asked Uncle Pogle.

"Well me lad, when he came back, he got off the last ferry when it docked, with a different dog. She was a fine beauty ah so she was; but she looked so frightened of him as well!" said O'Seanessy.

Uncle Pogle began to tremble and Tudor shook his head until his brandy keg came off and Uncle Pogle had a medicinal tot of brandy to steady his nerves.

"Can I ask you O'Seanessy; do you know what sort of breed of dog he had with him when he came back?" said Uncle Pogle.

O'Seanessy removed his trilby hat and scratched his head...

"Oh to be sure I have remembered now; she was a little brown sausage dog, but the name of the breed escapes me!"

Uncle Pogle went white as a ghost. "A Dachshund?" said Uncle

Pogle, as he stood up...

"Aye that do be it; a sort of long little brown sausage on Queen Anne legs!"

Uncle Pogle sat down again, stood up again and then sat down again, with his head in   hands....

"I think I can be helping you some more, so I do!" said O'Seanessy. "The white van had a name on the side so it did.... Henry Smythe-Jones; to be sure that was the name!"

Tudor Chops began to grumble to himself "Where have I heard that name before... Henry Smythe-Jones, Henry Smythe-Jones...!"

Uncle Pogle wondered what on earth Tudor was rambling on about. Tudor was spinning and growling.

"Calm down Tudor!" said Uncle Pogle. "Have a sausage while we think what to do...

"Sausage, sausage!" thought Tudor... "I remember, I remember Uncle Pogle!" said Tudor. "Henry Smythe-Jones is a dognapper, we have no time to lose, his name is not just Henry Smythe-Jones; he is a pirate and he is known as 'Captain Splints'

Uncle Pogle thanked O'Seanessy for his kindness and help.

After having a few words with the Inn keeper, who introduced himself as Donald O'Donnel; Uncle Pogle found out where the 'innocent looking' farm was, which belonged to Henry Smythe-Jones. Donald O'Donnel drew him a map. Uncle Pogle and Tudor Chops went in pursuit of 'Captain Splints'...

CAPTAIN SPLINTS

Henry Smythe-Jones had been arrested in Withernsea, where Tudor lived; after his pirate ship was found to be full of stolen dogs, all with the intention of being taken for breeding. The dogs had been rescued and went to a rescue in Wales, which was run by David and Myfanwy; two very loving and caring special fairies. They had all been found loving forever homes. Fairies can make themselves almost as big as Elves, or as tiny as they can be, whenever the need arises...

Tudor Chops told Uncle Pogle all about what had happened in Withernsea, on the East coast of Yorkshelf; and that everybody believed Captain Splints had been taken back to his home in Tahiti to be put in prison there, for many years...

Nobody knew that the evil pirate had already begun to set his puppy farm up over in Ireland...

Captain Splints had escaped and was now running a very uncompassionate puppy farm, pretending to be a nice dog breeder... he would look for advertisements where trusting people had asked for a good home for their dogs, for one reason or another, when they could no longer afford to feed them, or if someone had died...

Captain Splints in the guise of Henry Smythe-Jones would contact them; and wearing his fine and dandy clothes and pretending to care for dogs, he would convince the people that he would give their dog a very loving home...

In reality, his puppy farm was bad. It was full of stolen dogs which were being kept in tiny cages. All the female dogs were having puppies, for Henry Smythe-Jones, as he was known locally; to make a lot of money for him to live a life of luxury. He was also keeping some of the female puppies for himself so they could have even more puppies, once they became old enough. They would never see daylight, never see the sea, never walk on grass, and only had the contact of the evil Elf they knew as Captain Splints and his cruelty. They were all very sad, and some were quite poorly. Captain Splints didn't care. If they became of no more use to him, he had decided to take them a long way away to England and abandon them; and that was what he had done that very day when he tied a little Lhasa Apso up, known as number 9, by the side of a busy road and left her to die; leaving no trail behind him. That was when he had seen an opportunity and had attacked Uncle Pogle and stole Poppy in the little Lhasa apso's place. The Lhasa apso was no use to him anymore; she had a nasty skin condition and no way was Captain Splints ever going to pay out in costly vet bills, because Captain Splints hated dogs

DUSK

Uncle Pogle and Tudor Chops followed the route from the directions that the

Inn Keeper, Donald O'Donnel had given to them, at the Shamrock Inn...

Dusk was beginning to fall when Uncle Pogle and Tudor reached their destination.

What a facade of a big house met them. They could hear barking and howling and some whimpering coming from the rear of the property. A white van was parked in its driveway, slightly hidden by some bushes. Uncle Pogle moved some of the bushes to one side. On the side it read Henry Smythe-Jones...

"This looks like the place we are after!" said Uncle Pogle.

They crept silently to the back of the house. Henry Smythe-Jones could be seen sitting by the fire. He was eating a big juicy steak with a very sharp knife; and he was laughing to himself; he had no table manners what so ever, as he drooled over his steak...

"That stupid little mutt I took today will breed me some fine Dachshund puppies. It's taken me weeks to find a female for that male I got that had been roaming the streets hungry, eating out of the dustbins of the cafes and restaurants!"

Captain Splints chuckled to himself. He was now back in his pirate outfit, which he always changed in to in private...

Uncle Pogle wondered who Captain Splints was talking to. Tudor Chops crept

to the side of the house and then came back...

"He has nobody with him Uncle Pogle only his parrot in its cage, mimicking everything he says!" said Tudor.

We will just have to sit and wait Tudor until hopefully he falls asleep; and they stayed in some bushes by the rear window of the house until darkness fell and contemplated what they could do, to find Poppy.

SAUSAGE WEDNESDAY

Tommy O'Toole, the elder Irish Leprechaun leader, was sat by the fireplace oiling his shillelagh, when his waistcoat pocket began to vibrate. He took out his emerald green crystal of all seeing and peered into it...

His old friend Lionel Saynelf was calling out to him..
"Tommy O'Toole please put your wireless on!"

Quick as a flash, Tommy O'Toole sprang to his feet, and did as he had been

requested. An Elf spoke during a news flash...

"We now move over to the news desk, for a very important announcement from an Elf called Sidney Chops of Withernsea, who has contacted us!"

Tommy O'Toole waited patiently until Mr. Chops spoke:

"Our beloved dog Tudor Chops, who we have had, since adopting him as a puppy, has been missing from home for what seems like an eternity to my wife Kate and I. If anybody knows of his whereabouts please let us know. Tudor is a St. Bernard. He has a keg barrel around his neck with the name Tudor engraved on it. Tudor is a very unusual St. Bernard; he has much shorter legs than a usual St. Bernard dog. Tudor's daddy was a St. Bernard, but his Mummy was a cross breed. She was a St. Bernard crossed with a dog of unknown breed!"

Kate Chops had to take over from her Husband, as Mr. Chops was becoming

very upset...

"Tudor, if you're listening to me from anywhere, if someone has taken you into their home, please return home to us. Daddy and I didn't mean to upset you; we just need you home safe now with us where you belong!"

Tommy O'Toole looked into his emerald crystal and waited for it to vibrate and

glow... and Tommy O'Toole 'saw'...

Quick as a flash Tommy tuned in his special emergency 2 way radios...

"Come in Lionel Saynelf; come in please to Tommy O'Toole!"

COBWEB COTTAGE

Up in Scotland, in a cottage by Loch Ness; Lionel Saynelf heard his wireless making a strange bleeping noise it had never made before; however, Lionel
knew it would be an emergency if ever it bleeped, and he knew it would be Tommy O'Toole, because Tommy was the only one who was able to use it to contact anybody in an emergency... Lionel went over to the wireless and tuned in to the special code to speak to his caller...

"Hello Tommy, Lionel here – over!"

"I do be having no time to explain Lionel!" Said Tommy O'Toole "I got your message and listened to the wireless report from your friends Kate and Sidney Chops. I do be going to send me emerald green rainbow over, get on it without delay. Tudor Chops knows you and he will trust you; over and out!"

Tommy O'Toole was true to his word, as he always was. In no time at all Lionel was on the rainbow and covered in gold-dust as he dropped off the end of it; to find himself standing beside Tudor Chops and a very confused Elf; who had never seen the likes of magic before in his life!

Tudor Chops was so relieved to see Lionel Saynelf.

After some very quick introductions, Lionel was told the whole story...

Lionel had not noticed his little dog Hamish Mc.Tiddle had jumped onto the emerald rainbow with him, and he turned to find Hamish standing behind him, wagging his tail at Tudor Chops, his old pal from Withernsea.

They were all whispering, pondering how they were going to find Poppy and

free all the other dogs they could hear crying in pain...

THE SHAMROCK INN

Back at the Shamrock Inn, of which Tommy O'Toole's cottage had been aptly named many Leprechaun years ago; in honour of all his Granddaddies who had been entrusted with the emerald green crystal of all seeing, and all of who had frequented the Inn for their tankards of O'Guinessy, also known as 'black gold'; O'Seanessy had been talking about the days strange events. Shamrock Inn had been handed down the line to all O'Donnel Granddaddies, before Donald inherited it.

Donald O'Donnel had never met Tommy O'Toole, but he did hope that one day he would have the pleasure of his company

THE O'TOOLE SHILLELAGH

Tommy O'Toole was pacing up and down in Shamrock Cottage. His wife Victoria and daughter Tomasina Violet had gone over to the Isle of Man, to visit her old friends. Tommy was lost without them, and Percy the blue Manx cat was of no use to him what so ever in a crisis. Percy had merely opened one eye, grumbled under his breath at being disturbed, and went back to sleep!

18

Tommy had seen in his emerald crystal, all the goings on at the evil puppy farm being run by the so called Henry Smythe-Jones.

Tommy walked over to his shillelagh which always stood beside the fireplace in the cottage. It looked so lonely without the company of his wife Victoria's broomstick. Tommy needed some inspiration...

"Isaac Smudge where do you be hiding?" called out Tommy O'Toole.

"I do be here Daddy!" said Isaac, with a mouthful of sausage Wednesday casserole, which Victoria had prepared before she left for Barregarrow on the Isle of Man earlier that morning, on her broomstick with Tomasina.

"Isaac Smudge, it do be an emergency; are you coming me pet with Daddy to save some poor doggies from cruelty, and help Lionel Saynelf and Hamish Mc.Tiddle, alongside an Elf I do not be knowing, called Uncle Pogle?"

"Yeh Yeh Yeh!" said Isaac Smudge.

Tommy picked up his shillelagh. From experience he knew it may come in very handy if ordered to make itself become a cudgel. His shillelagh had saved Tommy on many occasions in the past; especially from highwaymen...

Tommy O'Toole looked into his emerald crystal, and he and Isaac Smudge

stole out into the now fast falling darkness, to be with the rescuers...
In no time at all, Tommy O'Toole, Lionel Saynelf and Uncle Pogle stood staring in disbelief at the pitiful sight that they could see, through the bars on the very small closed windows of the dog kennel, behind the facade of the house of Henry Smythe-Jones,

now known to be the evil Captain Splints.

The stench was nauseating, but it was no hindrance to them. These poor dogs

must be freed at any cost...

Hamish Mc.Tiddle began to growl. It was followed by Tudor Chops joining in. Isaac Smudge hid behind his daddy's shillelagh!

A rustling in the bushes alerted them. Both dogs dived into the bushes followed by Tommy O'Toole, Lionel and Uncle Pogle and Isaac Smudge! They kept very still and silent, waiting to see who the intruders were...

LANTERNS OF HOPE

IN THE DARKNESS

"This is the place!" said a familiar voice to the ears of Uncle Pogle and Tudor

Chops...

Uncle Pogle breathed a sigh of relief, as he saw O'Seanessy carrying a lantern, which was very dimly lit in the darkness.

More footsteps could be heard faintly following O'Seanessy's lead in the dim

light...

"I do be bringing just a few of me friends, ah so I do, from the Shamrock Inn!" whispered O'Seanessy.

All the Elves were wearing dark hoods so nobody present could see their faces

which were also covered with mud, to camouflage who they were...

Hamish Mc.Tiddle began to sniff the air, and then he wagged his tail; knowing

they were among friendly Elves. Hamish kept quiet...

Tommy O'Toole crossed his legs and did a jig in the air, as he bid his shillelagh to become a cudgel. The cudgel was placed outside the back door of the house, where Captain Splints had by now fallen fast asleep in his big captains chair, and he was snoring...

Tommy told the cudgel to guard the door until he came back for it. The cudgel trembled to acknowledge it had understood the orders of its master... if Captain Splints were to waken, the cudgel would have barred his way by doing its job, and nobody ever messed with the O'Toole shillelagh...

All the Elves had promised O'Seanessy not to speak, and they kept their promises as they went about their task.

One of the Elves had some bolt cutters, and as quiet as he could, he released the lock to the door of the kennel house. The smell almost made them all keel over as they quietly entered.

Once inside, lanterns were lit fully, and the sight that met them brought about such deep compassion.

Small cages were full of dogs. Their coats were filthy and all matted up. Some of the dogs had poorly eyes, others were whining with toothache, and some had very bad eyes. Their fur was so long and tangled, and it was hard to tell what some of the breeds were supposed to be...

Puppies were closely huddled hiding behind their Mother's. The

Mother's looked petrified. The only time they had contact with anybody from the outside world, was when Henry Smythe-Jones fed them their meagre scraps; which he stole every night out of the bins, of the cafes and restaurants that humans frequented.

Hamish Mc.Tiddle, Tudor Chops and Isaac Smudge ran to all the cages, and

calmed all the captured dogs down. Each one in turn became silent...

The hooded Elves set to work with their screwdrivers to remove the hinges on the doors of all the cages, as quickly and as quietly as they possibly could.

Uncle Pogle suddenly gave a sigh of relief. Running towards him was his little Poppy. So lucky to have only been there a short while. She was shaken but she never gave up hope of Uncle Pogle finding her.

Each dog and all the puppies were led outside to the freedom some of them had never known; but many had been stolen, and some had been strays thrown out by cruel owners, who did not want them once their novelty had worn off, or they had grown too big to afford to feed. Many were from the 'free to good home' advertisements; that Captain Splints read about, in various places.

Tommy O'Toole stood mesmerized.

"What on earth are we to do with all these poor dogs Lionel?" asked Tommy sadly.

"No worries Tommy!" said Lionel. "I know just the place for them all until loving homes can be found; or the owners of the stolen ones are traced!"

Hamish Mc.Tiddle appeared to be talking to himself. He was in full conversation with someone nobody else could see. Hamish was a psychic dog, and he had a spirit human friend called Peter. Peter had been the little boy of a lady called Elizabeth Turner, who had lived in Withernsea, in her cottage by the sea, known as Periwinkle Cottage. Peter had died in a drowning accident with his daddy when they had tried to rescue whisky, their King Charles Cavalier Blenheim spaniel. All three had drowned, leaving Elizabeth alone. Elizabeth had given Hamish Mc.Tiddle a loving home when she had found him on Withernsea beach, near her cottage. Sadly, one day, Hamish had been stolen from outside the cottage by some Elves. He had been found abandoned in Sherwood Forest and entrusted to Lionel Saynelf to be cared for. Elizabeth had since died, but not until she had found out Hamish was in the safe hands of Lionel, and in gratitude, she had left Periwinkle Cottage in Withernsea, to Lionel Saynelf. She wanted him to allow all kind persons, be they Elf or Human, to have a much needed holiday free of charge. That was how Lionel had met Kate and Sidney Chops, and their St. Bernard, Tudor...

Hamish ran over to Lionel...

"Write letter' woof woof, write letter, put in Hamish's collar, woof woof. Peter take to Wales to David and Myfanwy!" and Hamish spun round in happiness.

"Of course!" exclaimed Lionel, who just by a stroke of luck, had a pad and pencil in his pocket.

Dear David and Myfanwy,

Your help is needed urgently. A major rescue has just taken place in Ireland, at an evil puppy breeding farm. Some are very old, some are poorly, and many many puppies need some fairy magic and your love and care until they are well enough to be found homes, or their true owners.

Kind regards Lionel Saynelf.

"Tell them to await me emerald rainbow Lionel, of many shades of green!" said Tommy O'Toole, who was hoping he had enough gold-dust in his pockets for all the dogs to go at once!

So Lionel added a post script!

Hamish was given the letter in his collar, and he ran over to an invisible Peter...

Within no time at all, a gigantic emerald rainbow appeared...

TOMMY O'TOOLE SPEAKS

"COME SIT ON MY RAINBOW WHERE GOLD-DUST

APPEARS

YOUR PROBLEM BE DEALTH WITH

'TWILL ALL BECOME CLEAR!"

All the dogs rescued that night, except Poppy, shot over to Wales on the rainbow, where David and Myfanwy had made themselves taller, and were both waiting to take care of them all with love and kindness...
Captain Splints was beginning to wake up, ready to go scavenging the bins for the dogs dinners... little did he know that there would be no dogs to feed, and never would be again...

The rescuers from the Shamrock Inn began to depart. The Inn keeper Donald O'Donnel promised he would contact the local constabulary, who would be waiting for Henry Smythe-Jones also known as Captain Splints upon his return.

The Inn keeper, Donald O'Donnel told Tommy O'Toole how honoured he was to have met him at long last, and if ever he needed any help in the future, he only had to ask...

Tommy and Uncle Pogle were confused as to how they had known to come to

help with the rescue...

"I have had my suspicions for some time!" said Donald. I spoke to O'Seanessy and he gathered some of his friends who he could trust!"

Two of the hooded Elves remained; and one of them spoke...

"Come with us Uncle Pogle, and your dog Poppy. You can stay with us until you find somewhere to live in peace in Ireland, among friends here in Dublin.

Lionel Saynelf stood looking in disbelief as the hoods were removed of the two Elves and their faces wiped fairly clean. There in front of him stood Seamus O'Granary and his son Leonard; the Elves who had given Lionel a home when he had nowhere to go, after he had run away from home as a young Elf...

Tommy O'Toole returned home with Isaac Smudge and his shillelagh. He placed it back in its position by the fireplace in Shamrock Cottage. He sat in his armchair, satisfied that Lionel and Hamish Mc.Tiddle would get Tudor Chops home, safely to Kate and Sidney Chops in Withernsea.

"Well Isaac Smudge, your Mammy Victoria will never believe what happened today when she gets home tomorrow to be sure she will not!

"I'm hungry Daddy!" said Isaac Smudge.

"So do I be as well Isaac!" said Tommy; and they tucked into sausage

Wednesday casserole...

OVER TO ENGLAND ON THE FERRY

Lionel, Hamish and Tudor got off the ferry in England. They began to walk towards the train station for the next train to Withernsea.

It had been a very long night, and was just breaking dawn...

Lionel had eaten on the ferry, but Tudor and Hamish decided they were ready for some breakfast. They sat down on the grass verge beside a host of daffodils, and began to tuck in to their sausages...

Lionel heard a very low whimper coming from afar. He got up and walked towards the sound, but he could see nothing.

Right in front of Lionel appeared the emerald rainbow of Tommy O'Toole. It appeared over his head and off jumped Tommy.

"Oh me pet, me pet. The little darling O'Seanessy told us about last night, that Captain Splints had with him when he got on the ferry yesterday, was abandoned by him and left to die here in England!"

exclaimed Tommy "me emerald crystal did begin to vibrate in me waistcoat pocket, so it did!" In his broad Irish Leprechaun accent!

"Get your breath back Tommy!" said Lionel.

Tommy O'Toole calmed down...

"As I was saying; me crystal was vibrating something crazy, and when I did look into it, I saw the face of a little dog with Peter. Peter told me through me crystal, that her name is Bonnie. He told me that the little Lhasa apso girl is very poorly with a skin condition, and she is very nearby us now!" said Tommy.

"I did hear a noise Tommy, but so far I can't find her. It did sound like a dog whimpering in fear and discomfort. Who is the little dog called Bonnie?" asked Lionel.

"Now there we have it!" said Tommy O'Toole "Peter told me that Bonnie's mummy misses her so much, and so Bonnie would like the little Lhasa Apso to live with her, knowing her mummy will make sure she is loved and help her to get better!" said Tommy.

They began to search through the daffodils for the little dog who had never

been outside before in her life...

There was so much yellow in Tommy's crystal, when he tried to see if he could see her... the smell of the daffodils was over powering Hamish and Tudor's noses... but Tommy O'Toole had an idea...

LAVENDER AMONG THE DAFFODILS

Lavender 'Smeltworthy' O'Clack was in her garden, down in Tintagel Castle. She was gathering flowers and herbs for her special potions of ointments to heal the animals of the hedgerow and forests.

Lavender was a witch, but she was a caring witch full of love for animals. She also was the companion of Asgarde the last dragon and a good friend of Tommy O'Toole.

Lavender looked up to see the emerald rainbow of Tommy O'Toole. She knew instinctively that her help and knowledge was needed somewhere.

Lavender grabbed her faithful old broomstick, along with her bag of special ointments which she had lovingly made. She was about to climb onto the emerald rainbow when she heard the familiar roar of Asgarde, the last Dragon, coming from his cave...

"Lavender 'Smeltworthy' O'Clack, where do you think you are going?" roared Asgarde.

"I don't really know Asgarde!" exclaimed Lavender "but I know it is urgent, or Tommy O'Toole would not be sending his rainbow for me!" replied Lavender, who was trying to get onto the rainbow with all her things. She knew Tommy could only use his rainbow for emergencies and so she took her broomstick for the journey home...

Asgarde came out of his cave. He was in a good mood after his nap. He

walked over to Lavender and handed her one of his 'flame claws'...

"Use this wisely Lavender; I can only allow you the one!" said Asgarde.

Lavender thanked Asgarde and said she would return as soon as she possibly could, and she climbed onto the emerald rainbow, and in no time at all she arrived in the daffodil hedgerow...

"Ah there you do be me pet!" said Tommy, as Lavender dismounted at the destination. She was covered in gold-dust, but she didn't mind.

All was explained to Lavender. She thought for a while and then she uttered a magic spell, which had been taught to her by her tutor, Madam Oonah Dingbat O'Finn, at the witches' school she had attended, on the Giants Causeway, over in Ireland. All the spells uttered by witches and wizards, were carried on the whispers of the wind to the causeway to be stored in secret, hidden among the cobblestones of time...

Lavender, chanted a spell...

BRING IT NEAR AND MAKE IT CLEAR
LET THE LAVENDER BLUE

SO APPEAR...

The strong aroma of beautifully scented lavender could be detected in the

distance, among the daffodils...

"That blue haze is so very near to the busy road!" said Lionel "I hope we are in time, I can't hear the whimpering any longer!"

"Well don't despair!" said Lavender "perhaps the little dog has fallen asleep!"

The purple blue haze was approached very carefully and calmly by Lavender 'Smeltworthy' O'Clack. She asked Tommy and Lionel to walk slowly at a pace or two behind her.

Lavender stopped in her tracks. The sight that met her neared her to tears. The little Lhasa apso, with no name who had been tied up by Henry Smythe-Jones and left to die, was lying at Lavender's feet. Lavender brushed away some of the flowers carefully with her broomstick...

Hamish Mc.Tiddle and Tudor Chops went towards Lavender 'Smeltworthy' O'Clack, and shielded the little Lhasa apso from the road; as Lavender took out some ointment, and gently rubbed it into the itching sore skin of the little abandoned dog from the puppy farm...

Lionel gently untied the thick rope from around her neck and he picked her up.

"She is very thirsty!" said Lavender "I have some special liquid in my bag for de-hydration.!"

Lavender took out a syringe from her bag, and administered the liquid as Lionel held on to the little Lhasa apso, gently stroking her head. The little dog began to pick up. She had never in her life been stroked before, but she knew instinctively that she was safe and she actually liked it...

"That's all I can do!" said Lavender "but I do believe she will be fine in time!"

Lavender handed Lionel a few jars of ointment. She mounted her broomstick.

"It's going to take you a long time to fly back to Tintagel Castle, Lavender!" said Tommy. "I do be so sorry me pet, that I cannot send you home on my rainbow Lavender, but returning you home is not classed as an emergency!"

Lavender remembered the Flame Claw she had been given by Asgarde.

She put it onto her broomstick at the brush end, and as she called out goodbye to them all, the broomstick suddenly went off into the air like a firework rocket towards Cornwall... "Goodbye Lavender; thank you, and a safe journey home!" they all shouted, as Lavender could just about be seen far off in the sky....

Tommy O'Toole sent for his emerald rainbow, telling himself that it could be classed as an emergency, because they needed to get the dogs to Withernsea, home safely.

At the other end; Lionel was still holding onto the little Lhasa apso, as he and Tudor and Hamish slid off the rainbow onto Withernsea beach, just outside the gate of Periwinkle Cottage!

"What shall I do with her Tommy?" shouted Lionel, as Tommy and his rainbow

were fading back to Dublin...

"T'will all become clear Lionel, 'twill all become clear very soon, to be sure it will" said Tommy O'Toole... find the Mummy of Bonnie; 'twill all become clear....!"

Lionel found the keys hidden under the mat at the cottage door. He went inside, followed by Hamish Mc.Tiddle and Tudor Chops. He placed the little Lhasa apso down on a cushion, and Tudor and Hamish lay beside her to keep her company, and give her confidence that she was not alone...

After a good rest, and plenty of nice scrambled egg for the little Lhasa apso; who had strangely picked up the dish, and taken it to Lionel; Lionel said it was time to take Tudor Chops home.

The little Lhasa apso had never said a word, but Lionel knew in time, she would be able to communicate with Elves and fairies.

A WARM WELCOME

They all set off for the butchers shop in Withernsea, belonging to Kate and

Sidney Chops...

Sidney Chops was very quietly making beef and tomato sausages. He was remembering how they were Tudor's favourites, right from him being a puppy when they had adopted him. He was in the back preparation room, and he had silent tears running down his face. Kate Chops was sat with her distant cousin, who was visiting from a village called Driffield. They had not seen each other for many years. Kate's cousin had heard the news on the wireless about Tudor being missing from home. She had never met Tudor, but she had much empathy, as she had recently lost her own little dog.

"I'm sure that Tudor will soon come home Kate, if he can – somehow I just feel

it; so don't despair!" she said..
Lionel was thinking, as they walked towards the butchers shop...

"Tudor, can I ask you a personal question!" said Lionel.
Tudor nodded his head...

"Why ever did you run away Tudor?" said Lionel.

Tudor Chops looked at Lionel Saynelf... "They were going to send me to Coventry Lionel, and I didn't want to go. They said I was eating them out of house and home; so I thought that was the reason they wanted to send me there. Lionel... is Coventry a place where you have to go on a diet?" asked Tudor.

Lionel began to laugh; the little dog he was holding tightly on to had never

heard such a noise before, but she knew it was a nice noise...

"No Tudor; being sent to Coventry is when somebody is to be ignored until they decide to behave and change their ways, you silly sausage!" said Lionel.

"So you mean they were not actually going to send me away Lionel to a nasty place because they didn't want me, after all?" asked Tudor.

"No Tudor they weren't, but eating between your meals is not good for you is it. Your tummy is rather more rounded than the last time I saw you!" answered Lionel, kindly!

"Do you think Kate and Sidney will let me come home?" asked Tudor.

"I am positive they will Tudor my fine friend; but to be a good guard dog for the shop, you cannot be falling asleep all the time whilst you are on your guard duty. Eating what you shouldn't is more than likely why you sleep too much!" said Lionel.

Lionel stopped just before they entered the shop... "Tudor Chops, you may have done wrong, but what happened was meant to happen. Without you, all those poor dogs may never have been rescued, because at the time, only you knew that Henry Smythe-Jones was really Captain Splints in disguise. Tudor, you are a very brave dog!"

They all entered the butchers shop...

"SHOOOOOOOOOOOOOOOOOOOOOOOP!" called out Lionel "anybody in?" I have someone special who wishes to be welcomed home!"

Kate and Sidney Chops recognized Lionel's voice and rushed through to the

front of the shop...

"Tudor oh Tudor, you old slobber chops; where ever have you been, we have been so worried?"

Tudor Chops almost knocked his Mummy and Daddy over, as he jumped up them both and placed a paw on each shoulder; first licking the face of Kate, and then Sidney!

Kate and Sidney Chops listened intently, as Lionel told them the whole story...

"What a dear little dog she is Lionel!" said Kate Chops, as she went over to stroke the little Lhasa apso on the forehead, between her eyes and on her nose!"

Kate called out to her distant cousin, to come through and meet Lionel and Hamish, and of course Tudor Chops.

Kate's distant cousin came through from the butcher's kitchen and went straight towards the little Lhasa apso, which Lionel was holding.

"May I hold her please Lionel?"

Lionel handed over the little dog...

"I would love to take her home Lionel!" she said.

"I'm so sorry Mrs. Errrrr sorry I didn't catch your name, did I?" said Lionel.

"This is Merice, my distant cousin Lionel!" said Kate Chops "I'm sure she will give the dog a loving home!"

"I'm so sorry Merice, but I have to search for someone very special, as was told to me by Tommy O'Toole, the Irish elder Leprechaun of Dublin!" said Lionel.

Merice looked sad... "Yes, I have heard of Tommy O'Toole, elder of the Leprechauns Lionel. I understand he is a wonderful leader. I respect that he will know best!"

Kate Chops explained to Lionel that Merice had not too long ago, lost her old

dog when she had died and gone over the rainbow bridge...

"I suppose you could look after her until we find the lady Elf in question!" said

Lionel, who really felt for Merice in her sadness...

"I don't think I could part with her Lionel if I fostered her!" said Merice. "I know fosterers are worth their weight in a cauldron of gold, and I admire them greatly, but I don't think I could do that task!"

Hamish Mc.Tiddle began to spin around and wag his tail...

"Woof woof, Peter is here and he says look in your pocket Mrs. Merice!"

"I am your Aunty Merice!" said Tudor's new Aunty.

Merice put her hand in her pocket and took out a piece of paper...

She handed it over to Lionel and asked him to read it; and she was looking very confused, the note had not been in her pocket when she put her cardigan on that morning...

Lionel began to read...

I'M SO SORRY MUMMY BUT THEY CALLED ME

TO GO

I WAS SO VERY OLD

BUT I WANT YOU TO KNOW...

THE KINDNESS YOU SHOWED – I TOOK IT WITH ME

I'M HERE AND I'M SAFE
AND THIS IS MY PLEA...

LOOK AFTER THE LITTLE DOG AS A GIFT FROM ABOVE

SHE NEEDS YOU NOW TO SHOW HER YOUR LOVE...

I WILL ALWAYS BE NEAR YOU ALTHOUGH WE DID PART

PLEASE CALL HER DILLY AND GIVE HER YOUR HEART...

Love Bonnie xx

... and with that, a white feather floated down, and it landed on

Dilly's head!

....

If you ever see an emerald rainbow of many shades of green in the sky, and it's not even been raining, send thoughts of hope to Tommy O'Toole; because he will be undertaking an emergency task in a mission of mercy.

AND TOMMY O'TOOLE IS ALWAYS TRUE TO HIS WORD
I am Kim Saynor-Lomas, the author of THE SECRETS OF THE CHRISTMAS HEAD AND THE MAGIC OF THE FLAME CLAWS, where Characters from this book herein are taken from; and available on Kindle.

With thanks to

GLENN MARSHALL

Printed in Great Britain
by Amazon